KEEP YOUR PANTIES UP

AND YOUR SKIRT DOWN

BY DANGEROUS LEE

ALLEN COUNTY PUBLIC LIBRARY

DEDICATION

This book is dedicated to the memory
of my grandmother, Mrs. Mable Langston.

She taught me to *Keep My Panties Up and My Skirt Down.*

I love and miss you.

Mrs. Mable Langston
July 25, 1929-January 10, 2009

CONTENTS

Introduction

I didn't write *"Keep Your Panties Up and Your Skirt Down"* to be preachy or to give you the idea that I have never had unprotected sex. Before I became wise in the ways of HIV and other STDs, I participated in unprotected sex and I was infected with an STD. Luckily it was a curable STD, but I felt very dirty. I learned the hard way. I don't want you to learn the way I did.

Revealing my past STD status makes me feel naked and raw, but I think it's very important that I admit this within the pages of this book. I know I am not the only person in my circle of friends or family that has had an STD. Hell, for all I know, some of them are infected now!

I'm also sure that many of you reading this are, or have been, infected with an STD. For that very reason I am not ashamed to reveal my past STD status. I'm just like you! Today I am STD free and I plan to stay that way for the rest of my life. I always practice safe sex. I am anal about it. No pun intended.

"Keep Your Panties Up and Your Skirt Down" is a phrase that my grandmother said often to me and my other female cousins when we were growing up. Essentially she was telling us not to have sex. I would roll my eyes in embarrassment because I was so young and sex was the farthest thing from my mind.

It is wonderful advice. Sex is a great thing, a beautiful thing, but if you're not mature enough for the responsibility or properly educated on the bad things that can happen when you have unprotected sex, it can truly be an ugly experience.

I don't really fancy myself a great writer of erotica. Though as a teenager I and a friend used to write erotic stories with Michael Jackson

INTRODUCTION

in the lead; I never thought I would go beyond that and publish a book full of erotic tales.

I enjoy reading erotica like millions of people, especially books written by Zane. When she announced an open call for her anthology, *"Succulent: Chocolate Flava 2"*, I figured what the hell, I'm a pretty good writer so I gave it a shot and my short story titled *"Til' Death Do Us Part"* made the cut. I officially became a published writer of erotica. By the way, *Succulent* is a New York Times Bestseller. Not bad for my first time out the box!

"Keep Your Panties Up and Your Skirt Down" is more than suggestive sex for your pleasure. It has a deeper meaning and is geared to educate you, make you think about your actions, and even shock you a bit.

I am a certified Community Health Advocate and Testing Counselor at Wellness AIDS Services, Inc. in my hometown of Flint, Michigan. This book was conceived before my employment. I've been working at Wellness for close to two years, so this book is past its due date.

"Keep Your Panties Up and Your Skirt Down" includes many of my passions - love for my grandmother, love for black people, love of intimacy, love of writing, and my love of life. Sex is always best with passion. Enjoy!

Directions: Be tested for HIV after reading.

THE SAFE SEX KIT

> "If I love Jodi the way I proclaim, I need to man up and talk safe sex with her and also reveal a side of myself that could result with her foot in my ass. I could lose Jodi tonight. The mere thought of that pains me, but she has shown me real love and I want to thank her for that."

Jodi and I have been seriously dating each other for eight months and having salacious sex for two years. Like most people this century, we were instantly sexually attracted to each other and the deep feelings followed much later.

We gave ourselves the titles of boyfriend and girlfriend after realizing that we never wanted to have sex with anyone else for the rest of our lives. She put it on me like a voodoo curse and I assume I get her off in the same way because we vibe on every level.

I have been monogamous since we titled ourselves and Jodi says she has let go of all her other sex partners, but a recent conference I attended about HIV/AIDS in the black community has a brotha wiggin' out. My past sex life can compete with that of a porn star. I used to have sex no less than twenty times a week and much of it was unprotected with various partners.

I was the king of pull out and cum on face, titties, stomach, ass, ears or anywhere else you'd allow my babies to flow. I have also had sex with a few men. Jodi does not know about this and I consider myself a straight man without a doubt. I love women and I ain't no punk, but every once in a while, or full moon, I'd meet a dude that had a way

4

about him that I found appealing and I'd bend him over and treat him just like a bitch. When I had sex with men I always made sure to protect myself as if I was assuming they would infect me with their awesomely tight asses.

I do have some issues with my attraction to men, but Jodi has me caught up. I don't want any other man or woman. I want to seriously talk about safe sex tonight as we partake in hopefully one of kinkiest sexcapades we'll ever experience.

The conference on HIV/AIDS stated, among other things, that dental dams should be used every time I perform oral sex on a woman and flavored condoms should be used when giving head to a man. Jodi and I have never had protected sex and we've never had a reason to start. However, that was before I got a reality check.

If I love Jodi the way I proclaim, I need to man up and talk safe sex with her and also reveal a side of myself that could result with her foot in my ass. I could lose Jodi tonight. The mere thought of that pains me, but she has shown me real love and I want to thank her for that. If she does dip on me, I can move on with a new outlook on life, sex, and relationships.

I want to make this as romantic and as sexy as possible. The lights are dimly lit, Maxwell is playing, Riesling is on ice, and daisy petals are thrown about in the various places I plan to fuck her. Daisies are Jodi's favorite flower. If I had rose petals all over the house she would walk right back out the door before I could share anything with her.

I also cooked dinner. Oh yea, a brotha can cook! Mama taught me well. I am a nervous wreck. Jodi is due home from work any minute now and my dick is hard from nervousness and the simple thought of her walking through the door.

Usually when Jodi gets home from work she immediately kicks off her heels and throws herself on the couch with a huff. I am bathed, freshly shaven (all over), my skin smells of shea butter, and I am stark naked. She's gonna trip when she sees me. I have never done anything like this before.

I can hear her key enter the lock and pre-cum is beginning to slide from my tip. My heart is racing. Jodi enters the room and kicks her heels off. She sees me and stops in mid-step.

"What the hell?" is all she can manage to say as a smile spreads across her beautiful, mahogany face.

"Come to me," I command her. She obeys.

"What's all this about?" she asks looking around at the erotic scene. "Take off your clothes," I continue to command her.

"Your wish is my command," she says throwing her purse to the floor as she starts to remove her business suit.

My dick is diamond hard and at attention like an honorable soldier. Jodi starts to remove her fishnet stockings. I sit in front of her and gently take her hand to help her balance. I stand up and tenderly place her on the couch. I smoothly reposition myself on one knee to help her fully remove her stockings holding her legs open to see her glowing pussy. It's plump and ready for me.

Jodi used to be so self conscious that she wanted to bathe before every sex session. I told her a man likes to taste a woman's real flava and a lil' funk aint never hurt anybody. Here she stands in her after work stressed glory, naked as the day she was born with the smile of a Cheshire cat.

"To what do I owe this exciting new surprise?" she asks.

"I want to play Show and Tell. Sit back and I will explain. You can ask questions as I go along."

Jodi is giddy with excitement, so unassuming. On the coffee table behind us I have created a safe sex kit. There are dental dams, water based lubricants, flavored latex condoms, her favorite dildo, and other naughty goodies. We love toys. In fact, it dawns on me that she has used a strap on with me in the past. Maybe she won't have a problem with my interest in men after all.

"Do I see condoms? We never use condoms!" she stated accusingly closing her legs and standing up with an attitude. My dick is sinking.

"Sit down baby and just let me tell you what I've learned recently."

She sits down with her arms crossed and has a look on her face that just made my dick completely soft. "Look, I know what you're thinking, but I'm not cheating and I'm not accusing you of cheating. It's nothing like that. Trust me," I plead still on one knee. She eases off the attitude a bit and relaxes her face muscles.

I get up to pour some wine. You have to remember that I am naked because I forgot. Jodi and I are so comfortable with each other that sometimes we walk around the house naked for the entire weekend. I imagine this is what life was like B.C.

Anyway, my boy is hanging at my thigh and my well-shaped ass muscles can't wait to be slapped. Yes, my ass is well-shaped. I take damn good care of myself. So does Jodi. We met working out. Damn, my dick is getting hard again!

I return with the wine and Jodi has a big smile on her face and her chocolate legs are wide open. My dick is almost at full mast by the sight of her brilliantly white teeth and swollen clit.

"Drink some and loosen up," I say passing her a flute full of wine.

"Damn, you're bossy tonight. I like it!" She takes a swig as I down mine in one gulp. I'm keeping a steady eye on her pussy. It's glistening for my attention.

"OK, it's time to play Show and Tell, but first I want to let you know just how much you mean to me, how much I love you, and how I want us to be together forever."

As I'm saying this, I wonder if she thinks I'm gonna propose marriage with all this lovey dovey shit I'm talking. Jodi is taking sips of her wine and is instinctively rubbing her clit with her free hand. I am officially at my full ten inches, but I am starting to get side-tracked.

I grab a strawberry flavored dental dam and some lubricant from the coffee table and continue my speech inching back to her on my knees. "I learned that black people are affected by HIV more than anyone else in this country. Though you and I are monogamous we haven't always been," I say making eye contact with a wink as I rub lubricant on her superb pussy. She flinches but is rolling with what I'm bringing. She drinks the last of her wine and lets the glass drop lightly on the couch.

Jodi is listening with anticipation but quickly lets me know that talking about STDs during sex is not very sexy at all. I know that, but I am gonna make it sexy come hell or high water, to prove a point.

"I have never had an HIV test, have you?" I ask. She nods. Her body is supple and more relaxed. Quite frankly, she has a buzz, but she is definitely alert to what I am saying and doing to her. "Oh, you have! I assume the result was negative?" She nods again. "I'm sorry I've never had a test. I really am. I could have exposed you to a virus without knowing it."

I am starting to feel guilty and I'm worried that I might be infected. My boy is going south again. This shit could give me blue balls.

Jodi lovingly strokes the hand I am pleasing her with. "It's OK baby. Don't feel bad. I had the test done when we started dating. We can get another one together." She coos with sex sounds in the background of her words.

I put the strawberry flavored dental dam on her pussy and aim my tongue towards it. "What is that?" she asks before I can make contact.

"It's a dental dam and it's the safest way to lick your pretty pussy." I start to give her head. There is no need to ask her if she likes it because her body is talking to me. I think she may be enjoying it more because I am able to do things to her that I can't do without a barrier. I am grazing my teeth across her clit and experimenting with something that I plan to name the "clit pop". I can't give all my secrets away. Use a dental dam and create your own tricks.

Jodi is going crazy. In between my tongue and teeth tricks I am dropping STD facts and informing her of various types of protection. This may not seem appealing, but I'm so excited that I just came on the floor. Jodi loves it too. "Teach me baby" seems to be her trademark phrase for the night. She has already cum twice and I changed the dental dam both times. The strawberry flavored dental dam is my favorite so far. Not once have I put my mouth on her naked pussy, though I'd love to rub my face in it.

I start to finger her pussy using a finger condom. Our eyes are locked and our breath is synchronized in a quick rhyming beat. God, I love sex with this woman! She is wildly gyrating her pussy on my fingers. If my fingers could cum they would fill her up immediately.

"If I told you I've had sex with a man what would you think?" I blurt out. I feel like I had to do it this way. There are so many emotions going through me right now. I want to cry.

Her gyrating has slowed a bit and I can tell by her expression that she wants to spit in my face, but she simply states "I would not like it, especially if it was while we were together". Her gyrating has completely stopped, but I'm keeping my fingers inside playing with the area directly below her G spot.

"No, it wasn't while I was with you, baby." Jodi removes my fingers from her pussy.

"Oh, so is that what tonight is about? You want to tell me you're gay?" She's officially pissed.

Damn, I have just ruined the mood. My boy is deflated yet again.

"No baby, I'm not gay. I guess you can call me bisexual, but you're all I need," I am begging her to understand. Jodi is a non-judgmental woman and she isn't homophobic, but she has a right to be upset. A man should let his woman know about things like this up front and vice versa.

Instead of slapping the shit out of me or cussing me out, she has decided to take control. "Get off your damn knees and sit down!" she angrily orders me. I obey, but I have to admit I am a little bit scared. I like it rough, but damn.

Jodi walks over to the coffee table and grabs a grape flavored condom. Her ass cheeks are visibly wet with her pussy juices. I glance down at myself to see my boy inching back up. On her very short walk back, I admire her swollen breasts and tight abs. The look on her face is that of a chick on a mission.

She grabs the lubricant from the floor and spreads some across my almost fully erect dick. The cold sensations combined with her warm hands make my dick quickly rise for the third time tonight. It's a painful sensation but my baby is stroking nice and slow as I lay back and close my eyes, sucking my lips into my mouth with my teeth letting muffled moans escape my throat.

"Look at me!" she demands. My eyes fly open and my head pops up at her command. Jodi continues to stroke me as our eyes lock for the second time. This was our way of being totally connected during sex, our thing, and if it didn't happen the sex was not spiritual to us.

"Can a man stroke your dick better than this?" Jodi growls.

"Hell no," I sigh.

She's going at it with brisk force. She's not doing the usual tip in mouth scenario. She is starting to get into this safe sex game. I cum again.

She continues to rub my aching dick as warm cum oozes onto her hand. She usually likes to taste it, but she is definitely being a good girl tonight.

Surprisingly, my dick is still hard as a cast iron skillet. Now she is placing the grape condom on me ever so gently and correctly so that there is room at the tip for the next bundle I am about to drop. She slaps my dick in her mouth. Oh lawd! Her tongue, the rubber, and the lubricant mixed with my cum is a new but pleasing sensation.

I sit up so I can get a better view of her head skills. Jodi is definitely performing for me. Our eyes lock for a magical third time as she takes all ten inches into her mouth while caressing my balls. "I love you." I mouth to her.

"Can a man suck dick better than me?" Jodi asks with a mouth full of meat. I hesitate. Let me tell you, men can suck a mean dick. Don't women say the same thing about lesbians? They have a pussy so they know what to do with it, right?

Jodi did give the best head out of all the women I'd had sex with but I knew better than to go there on the men tip. She was asking a rhetorical question as far as I was concerned. She wants an answer, but it won't necessarily be the entire truth in this case.

"You give the sweetest head, baby," I managed to get out. I am about to bust again. She removes the condom that she used to give me head and replaces it with a lubricated condom. She sits her juicy, wet, and ready pussy on my dick. I am amazed that she has lasted this long without my dick or her favorite dildo inside of her. Jodi was worse than a man sometimes. She definitely didn't need foreplay. Jodi is all about getting her fuck on.

She's riding me aggressively and we're getting into a nasty rhythm, almost a competition to see who can get freakier with their hip action. She leans into my face and licks my lips. It's the first time that a tongue has touched raw skin tonight.

I open my mouth to take her tongue inside and it becomes obvious that neither of us has had dinner. I really could eat her sexy ass alive. She is delicious from head to toe.

Our mouths part as her pussy sends me into whine mode. Ooooh, she is so tight and her stroke is on point! She's licking my face, ears, neck, and nipples as she rides me like a possessed cow girl. I cum hard! I hold her tight as she keeps a very slow rhythm making sure nothing is left in my sack. Woo, lawd, this woman. Damn!

"So, you like dick, huh?" she asks bending over to expose her willing ass. "Or do you like ass?" We've never had anal sex so I am a little hesitant to go there, but a clear view of her ass, gives me a second opinion.

"If a man can take it so can I," she hisses. I know her ass is Zip Lock tight so I am ready to take it on a joy ride. I grab the lubricant and gently began to massage her ass. I decide that using my fingers is best for her first time experimenting with ass play. My full ten inches could kill her; or at least that's what my ego is telling me. Obviously Jodi agrees because I am laying it down with my fingers and she's not ordering the dick.

After Jodi cums she speaks softly, "Thank you for being honest with me. I know it was hard to tell me about your attraction to men. It was hard to hear, but I can accept it and I can accept you. We should have had this talk before I had my HIV test. But, just so you know I've always wanted a threesome with two men." We both let out an evil chuckle.

I sit her down in my lap like a baby, and she was my baby so it was okay. We embrace tenderly for quite some time without saying a word.

"Thank You," I finally tell her. I am such a little bitch. My eyes fill with tears. None had a chance to drop because my baby made me laugh by jumping up and proclaiming her hunger for food.

"What did you cook for me?" Her ass bounced as she ran to the decorated kitchen table. I run behind her.

"Crab legs, but they're cold now. Let's just get to the dessert," I say motioning to the covered dessert tray. "Open it," I order her.

When she opens it two at-home HIV tests I bought from Walgreens are revealed. She smiles with mischievous delight and sashays back towards the living room.

"Where are you going?" I ask.

"I can't believe you let those crab legs get cold. You have to eat my pussy as punishment while they're warming up." Eating her pussy is supposed to be punishment, was she serious? She returns to the kitchen holding a dental dam in one hand and her strap on in the other. We are both in for a treat.

THE SAFE SEX KIT

This time the crab legs almost burned.

Our HIV tests came back negative. We both also got complete physicals by our respective general physicians and received clean bills of health. Well, not fully, we both need to watch our cholesterol levels.

I almost forgot the most important part. After we got our HIV results I proposed, she said yes, and we had the nastiest unprotected sex I've ever experienced. She still made me use a dental dam to eat her pussy though.

What can I say, Jodi knows what she likes and who am I to deny her?

SELF LOVE AND PAIN

---

*"Before he got himself cleaned up and
drug free he was an intravenous drug
user who shared needles with other
IV drug users."*

I am in love with myself. That's right; I turn my damn self on. As I stand here in my black lace bra and panties I am turned on by my full-figured image. I love my body. I've had this love affair before, but now it's permanent.

Unfortunately, my boyfriend died of AIDS. I am HIV negative. We always had safe sex. I knew he had AIDS, and I also knew how to protect myself. Winston was honest with me from the very beginning and I made the decision after dating and getting to know him for three months that I wanted to severely fuck him until the day AIDS took his life.

Doesn't sound romantic? That's because you're the type that believes in fairy tales. Has a knight in shining armor ever tried to get your phone number? Hell no! Real knights are usually in rusted armor that require several cans of oil.

When I met Winston he appeared healthy as a race horse. Before he got himself cleaned up and drug free he was an intravenous drug user who shared needles with other IV drug users. By the time I met him he was a very successful business man looking to make each moment count.

SELF LOVE AND PAIN

He told me he never thought he would have sex again, but if he did meet a woman that gave him a great mind fuck, he would approach her and honestly tell her his HIV status. It was sort of a test that he had given himself and if he passed this test he was an honorable man and could walk away with dignity even if he was told to fuck off.

I was both intrigued and scared as hell when Winston casually told me he had AIDS. I knew all the wrong things about HIV. I liked him enough to learn the truth about HIV and I grew to love him in the process.

I had my eye on Winston weeks before we formally met. When he approached me my panties let off a scent that if translated, would say hell yes. He didn't inform me of his status until the subject of sex rolled from my eager lips. He playfully dangled his HIV test results in my face. I still have that piece of paper and carry those results in my purse every day.

You have to see the paperwork these days ladies and gentlemen. If someone says they don't have HIV ask them to prove it. Anyone with a negative result does not have a problem sharing the news or showing the paperwork. If they act shady when you ask for proof, keep on walking or pull up your panties or drawls if you took it that far. As a matter of fact, test results can be fabricated so the best thing to do is get tested together and grab some condoms on the way out.

We had very stimulating talks about safe sex and the ways he could safely bring me to orgasm many times without penetrating me with his dick. I've never been so turned on by learning. He was definitely not a shit talker. He was the best I'd ever had and I hadn't completely had him yet. I wanted to be tested so that we could safely go further in the bedroom.

We were together six glorious years and one fine day he became severely ill and seven months later he was gone, buried. I cannot give myself to anyone else. Not yet, maybe never. He was my soul mate. He loved me with his whole soul and I miss that. He helped me to

see myself in ways that I never knew existed by taking the time to appreciate every inch of my curvaceous body and deeply probing my mind.

As I look at myself in this full length mirror it is in Winston's honor. Before he died he told me that whenever I felt erotic that I should wear his favorite lingerie and imagine his hands, his scent, and his glorious dick inside me.

His hands are now mine and as I touch myself I can feel Winston making the motions. It is his spirit that is running fingers through my hair. The tingle in my pelvis is his sexual sprit running though me. I know he's in heaven because this feeling is divine. That may sound corny, but truth is truth. I am not over him and I never will be if I can get this feeling without the presence of a live man.

I remove my black lace bra and I am seeing myself through Winston's eyes. I pull my right breast to my mouth and plant kisses on it and tickle the nipple with the tip of my tongue and end it with a perverted pinch. Winston used to pinch my nipples this way. I like a little pain with my pleasure.

My hands trembling, I grab the baby oil from the nightstand and douse my breasts with it and watch them gleam as I rub the oil into my skin. I'm ignoring my pussy on purpose the way Winston used to.

I turn around in the mirror to adore the view of my buxom ass. You can set a small tea set on my ass and it will hold it perfectly in place. The curve of my back on the way to my ass is immaculate and should be in Guinness World Records for that reason. My skin, flowing sweetmeat of various shades, is darkest around my ass.

I don't work out often but my legs and arms are athletic. "I am kinda cute," slips from my lips and a voice inside me says - Cute my ass! You're legendary. Your beauty cannot be matched, not even by a child that you bare.

Winston told me that once and I swear it made me fall in love. I had never heard such angelic words. I do hope it was an original line and not one that he's used to get panties off other women in the past.

After admiring myself I plop down on my oversized cushy chair that I bought just for these special moments. I never needed music, special lighting, or candles to get in the mood for this experience. Winston just had to enter my spirit at the right time of day and no matter where I was or what I was doing, I would head home for privacy.

Today I was having dinner with my mom and had to fake an oncoming migraine to get away. I requested a doggy bag, gave my mom a kiss, left a generous tip, and here I am. I have a rumble in my tummy but my hunger can wait until my sexual needs are satisfied. Besides, food is always better after sex. Cigarettes can kill.

There is a nice wet circle in my panties warning me it is time to ease the pain. As I anxiously lift my shapely legs, gracefully I remove my panties one leg at a time, with pointed toes, giving myself a show in the mirror making more juices flow from my impeccable pussy. Hey, Winston used to call it impeccable so that's what it shall be.

I place my panties to my nose and inhale the yummy scent. I close my eyes and adoringly ease my middle finger inside my impeccably tight pussy. Winston was gifted at finger fucking. Before him most men thought if they just poked their rough, non manicured fingers in and out of my pussy, they were doing something special. The horrible thing is, my silly ass used to enable the pathetic performance by pretending that it was getting me off.

My finger feels strong the way Winston's did. I add my pointer finger to the madness and it makes me squirm in my seat. I open my eyes slightly to continue watching myself in the mirror. I savor what I see. I use my other hand to play with my shapely breasts and to spank my clit.

I am almost there, shaking, but I don't want to cum yet. I place a leg over each arm of the chair to get a good view of my exquisite pussy. I remove my fingers and lick them dry. From the cushion, I pull out the special box that housed my favorite vibrator. That goofy ass Dick in a Box song enters my mind from the popular Saturday Night Live skit. Unfortunately, I knew the lyrics and sang them proudly.

My Dick in a Box was almost the same length and girth as Winston. I shopped around for months with a Polaroid of Winston's firm dick to find the closest replica. I finally found one in his favorite color, red. My favorite part of the vibrator are the specks of gold glitter covering the tip.

I lick my lips as the vibrator approaches my throbbing pussy walls. I set it on the lowest vibrate level to tease. I close my eyes again and flashes of Winston and I having passionate sex, making love, and fucking each other on the bed, the floor, in his car in various positions make me cum immediately.

I almost wore myself out on the lowest vibrate level! Aint that a bitch? I want more. I turn it up to the highest vibrate level and use both hands to shove it in and out. This time I feel like I have help.

I can feel the pressure of male hips against each thrust. Winston is here with me. I have finally made it to the plane of spirit and living cumming together. I move the vibrator in and out quickly with long strokes. My toes are curling, my breathing is heavy, and I am sweating heavily. I can smell Winston's scent and feel his breath on my neck. I keep my eyes closed for fear that opening them will make the whole scene disappear like a dream.

At this very pivotal moment the battery dies and my phone rings, startling me to death. My eyes jolt open and "Shit!" bitterly escapes my mouth. I remember that I didn't take the phone off the hook before getting started. That was mistake number one, being too anxious.

I pull the vibrator from my pussy and pop it in my mouth to give it one last suck for shits and giggles, but it was out for the count. I quickly rise from my chair to see my mother's number on the caller ID. No doubt calling to see if her baby was okay.

I answer winded. "Yes, mom I'm fine. I don't have any pain

medication in the house so I'm on my way back out to buy some Ibuprofen and batteries." "Batteries?" mom asked confused.

I giggle sinfully.

AN
HONEST
HO

"Vashti learned at an early age that
she held true power between her legs
and was on a mission to make every
man she fucked weak in the knees."

Vashti is a ho, a good ho, a safe ho if that makes any sense. She'll fuck a married man, a minister, or your boyfriend; it doesn't matter. If she wants him, nine times out of ten, she will get him. Especially the ministers, they're always extra freaky. It must be the God in them.

Vashti is gorgeous, sweet, and sex crazed. Think of her as a cross between Grace Jones and Princess Grace. The one thing about her that you can respect is the fact that she always has safe sex and if a brotha is not down for it, he has to step aside with a stiff dick in hand. Most importantly, Vashti is honest about her HIV positive status.

She wasn't a street ho or at the Bunny Ranch waiting for men to drop their seed for a fee. She was a professional at sex; nasty, low down, filthy sex. Vashti knew there was power in exceptional fucking. Her dad promising to do anything her mom asked of him with the promise of pussy at sundown was an indication of that fact.

As a teenager Vashti also overheard a group of male peers admit that as long as a chick is fucking them when, where, and how they want, there was nothing they would refuse her. She concluded that men were very easy to please.

Vashti learned at an early age that she held true power between her legs and was on a mission to make every man she fucked weak in the knees. Vashti may not have dressed the part of a ho and wasn't paid for her services, but she played the role by definition. She also never fucked the same man twice. That's right, if you got her once you were lucky or unlucky depending on how you dealt with the situation.

The story behind Vashti's current safe sexual behavior lies in her volatile behavior of the past. She would use sex as a weapon having it often and with many different partners unprotected. Men would develop feelings for her and she would use that to destroy them with her sexual prowess and they'd never hear from her again. Lady GaGa must have written Bad Romance after a bout with Vashti. Sounds dramatic, but Vashti is a bad bitch!

However, she had forgotten what she learned as a young girl regarding a man doing anything for you if he was pleased sexually. Besides, what can you gain when you disappear immediately after a man cums? Not a damn thing, except a preventable and incurable STD such as HIV.

As you can imagine, Vashti's fan club grew quite large over the years. She never gave or received a phone number or any other contact information from her "victims" and the sex always took place in a hotel or at the man's home, even if he was married. Men stalked her and approached her constantly begging for another chance. Women hated her and secretly wanted to possess her power, but Vashti knew how to handle her business, or so she thought.

On one occasion as she scoped out her next "victim", a wannabe victim with stank breath and an ugly cold sore that she had turned down more than a few times whispered in her ear, "One day you're gonna give that pussy to the wrong man and he's gonna make you pay".

After she swatted him away like an annoying gnat, she gave his statement some thought then shook it off. "It hasn't happened yet and quite frankly I'm not convinced that any man can have that much power over me."

At that time Vashti knew one little safe sex tidbit regarding letting his mouth near her pussy. His cold sore could leave her with genital herpes, but she wouldn't have wasted so much as a decent dental dam on his janky ass to prevent it from happening.

When Vashti learned that she contracted HIV she wanted to end her life and felt unlovable and most importantly, unfuckable. She foolishly wanted to make every man pay for her irresponsible behavior. She was informed by her caseworker that before she had sex with anyone in the future that she would have to tell them her HIV status or it would be considered a felony and she could spend time in jail. This scared the hell out of Vashti. Would she ever fuck again? Was she still sexy? Would men deny her?

She took a year away from the ho life, educated herself on HIV and other STDs, dealt with the lengthy process of informing her past partners of her status, and relocated to a place where no one knew her. She had fucked most of the men within a fifty mile radius, so if she was to start over properly, it had to be in a new town in another state.

After a year of only pleasing herself, she decided it was time to get some dick. She promised to be honest about her status and protect herself and anyone that she had sex with. If a man insisted on not using protection she would slap his dick to the side and move on to the next. There was always a next in line and the last thing she needed was another STD to further weaken her immune system. Her T cell count was well above two hundred and she didn't currently need to be on any HIV medication. She ate healthy, worked out, and was in great shape.

One hot summer night Vashti felt like checking out a dance club called Pulse. Hopefully dancing up a sweat would get her sexual pulse pumping. She got dolled up the way she did in her ho days and decided to give flirting with HIV a shot. If she saw someone that caught her eye she would approach, if not, she would people watch and order her favorite drink all night, grape vodka.

Pulse was a spot a half hour away from her new home. She heard it was the ultimate spot to meet high class men, so she had to be in attendance.

Vashti decided that she would start to get more in return from men. No more of that fuck 'em and leave 'em nonsense. That attitude left her with HIV. Now she wanted to leave with a little TLC and possibly an SUV.

As soon as she stepped into the club she turned heads and women were already smacking their lips in disgust and intimidation. Vashti smirked at the ridiculous scene. It was one that she was all too familiar with, but hadn't experienced in over a year.

She had almost forgotten that she was HIV positive then snapped back to reality when a man she immediately wanted to fuck caught her eye. He appeared to be hanging with his boys at the bar. He looked like Billy Dee and Diana Ross' love child. Vashti elegantly slid next to him and ordered a drink.

"Grape Vodka shot in a dirty glass, please". She always wanted to say that corny ass line. The bartender knew she was full of shit. He fully intended to give her a clean shot glass. Pulse was too classy for that mess.

The order caught the attention of the man she had her eye on. "Hey, put that on my tab," he shouted to the bartender as he turned to face Vashti. Their eyes met.

"Thanks," Vashti said cutely.

"A dirty glass, huh? I've never heard that line outside of the movies," he said with a chortle.

"Me either." Vashti snickered back.

She liked this guy. This was not good. How in the hell was she gonna have control if she really liked him?

"So, what's your name?" Vashti asked.

"Rick." He shot back.

"Rick rhymes with big dick. I wonder if he's packing?", Vashti imagined.

"So, can I get your name?" Rick inquired.

"Oh, I'm sorry. I'm Vashti," she extended her hand.

He tenderly embraced her hand and placed a light kiss on it. "Yea right, when did men start kissing hands again?" Vashti asked. He saw the incredulous look on her face and he began to laugh.

"I saw it in a movie once and I've always wanted to do that too."

"You're funny. I like that," Vashti oozed loudly before she could control her reaction.

The bartender placed the grape vodka shot in front of her. Vashti downed it all in one gulp. "Damn, does the dirty glass make it easier to swallow?" Rick asked in astonishment.

The grape vodka along with the thought of swallowing quickly went to Vashti's head and she took a trip into her own world:

Vashti carried all the tricks of the trade; condoms, water based lubricants, dental dams, but her favorite was the female condom. The female condom can be a little tricky to insert, but Vashti perfected a way to make the experience very erotic and stimulating to the male eye.

She planned to carefully tear open the female condom packet with her teeth and alarm Rick with this odd form of protection that most people have never used much less seen up close. As she pleased herself with one, two, and then three fingers she would tastefully place the female condom in her slick pussy. She would then beckon Rick over with the curve of her wet pointer finger and he would do as he was told followed up with an intense round of fuckin'. That was the plan in her mind.

Rick noticed Vashti daydreaming and decided to bring her back to reality with these words - "Achashveirosh ordered Vashti to appear at the feast unclothed so that he could show off her beauty to his entire kingdom." Vashti's head whipped in Rick's direction with a look of awe on her face.

No one ever knew the story of the woman she was named after. This fact almost set her panties ablaze, but she also felt something above the belt and near her chest getting warm, her heart.

"Would you behead me if I told you I was HIV positive?" Vashti eagerly asked.

"Not even at the advice of Minister Memuchan," Rick answered. Vashti blushed and became a beautiful ruby shade of caramel.

Maybe a ho can become an honest housewife, or at least a bona fide girlfriend.

ELDERLY AND EDIBLE

"One lazy Sunday morning during
breakfast Rion, Glen's wife, sat
down a box of pubic hair dye
called Betty for Men on
the table in front of him and
remained silent. "What is this?"
Glen asked staring over the rim of
his glasses. "Read the box",
Rion demanded in a tone that
accused him of being dense."

Glen's wife of thirty-five years refused to go down on him when she spotted a few grey pubic hairs. Sadly, oral sex was the only form of sex that Glen received from his wife in the last nine years and even that didn't happen often. Why vaginal sex had ceased to exist was never discussed and neither one of them wanted to rock the already shaky boat so they never brought up the subject. If she was fucking someone he must have been younger and all of his pubic hairs were equally as youthful.

The pubic incident happened about six months ago and the only sexual advance Glen received from his wife since then was an occasional unwanted view of her strutting around in her holey granny panties and bra that didn't match.

Glen wasn't very upset that he no longer received head from his wife because she lacked proper skills and acted as if she was doing him a favor with each lousy slurp.

One lazy Sunday morning during breakfast Rion, Glen's wife, sat down a box of pubic hair dye called Betty for Men in front of him and remained silent.

"What is this?" Glen asked staring over the rim of his glasses.

"Read the box," Rion demanded in a tone that accused him of being dense.

"Color for the hair down there," he read aloud. Are you serious?" Glen asked removing his glasses and giving Rion a shitty look.

"Yes darling, if you ever want your dick sucked again I suggest you use it," Rion stated matter of factly without making eye contact.

"You know, you have a lot of damn nerve. Your pussy may not be grey yet, but it's definitely not mouth watering either," Glen retorted.

Rion took a deep breath and smacked her lips. "Seeing as how you rarely pay attention to my pussy I'm surprised you still know what it looks like," she grumbled giving full attention to her ham and cheese omelet. Glen excused himself from the table after slapping the Betty for Men box to the floor. Rion continued to devour her omelet.

It was a shame that after all these years it came down to a few grey pubic hairs and a stale vagina. Glen was an older man, but he definitely had sexual needs. He had been eyeing his friend Leroy's daughter, Tina, who had just turned twenty-one, at the last few family get-togethers. She was a hot little thing. Women didn't present themselves like she did in his day unless they were whores.

In this day and age all one had to do was turn to BET to see a cornucopia of women dressed like Tina. Glen figured it was a sign of the times.

Glen never said anything other than a nonchalant hello and offered Tina a polite hug each time he saw her. She would always hug Glen a little too tightly and glide her hand across his ass. Glen would instantly get a hard on.

Rion would be nearby watching giving Glen the evil eye. Truth be told, he was more worried about his friend Leroy kicking his ass if he knew the things he wanted to do to his daughter.

Glen knew Tina worked at a McDonalds a few miles from his home, so he decided to stop by and see if she was working while his wife was out of town on a shopping trip. He hadn't worked out what he would do or say. He decided to let her take the lead and if she threw out the bait he was definitely gonna bite that ass.

Luckily Tina was working the front register. She looked totally different in her work uniform. She actually looked her age. Still sexy and very fuckable, but she looked like a young lady.

"Hey, Mr. Glen can I take your order?"

"Hi sweetheart, I'll have a number three and your phone number." Tina giggled.

A few of her co-workers showed disgust at the all too familiar cheesy giggle she let loose each time a man flirted with her, which was just about every other horny dude that stepped to her register.

"What drink would you like with that?" Tina asked

"You decide, young lady," Glen replied.

"OK, a Coke it is." Tina lightly licked her lips without losing eye contact sending sex signals to Glen's pants.

Glen gave her a fifty dollar bill and told her to keep the change. She seductively handed him his food and a receipt with her phone number on the back. Glen returned to his car to enjoy his meal. As he ate Glen became hypnotized by what was written on the receipt: I get off in an hour. Wait for me.

Getting off was exactly what Glen had in mind.

More than an hour passed and Glen had fallen asleep. Tina's knock on the window startled him. She stood there posing an innocent smile. He got out of the car like a lustful gentleman and escorted her to the other side to open the passenger door. There was awkward silence and uncomfortable fidgeting when he joined her inside on the driver's side.

"So, what are we gonna do now?" Michael Jackson's Thriller popped into Glen's head because that same question was asked before Mike turned into a werewolf and ate Ola Ray's ass up.

"Mr. Glen!" Tina snapped.

"Sorry, my head was somewhere else. Please forgive me

sweetheart."

"It's OK. I know a quiet spot we can hit and your head can be somewhere more appropriate. Drive and I'll be your human GPS," Tina declared.

Damn! No questions asked? This was too easy.

The roar of the engine sent more sex signals to Glen's pants as he started the car. This was really happening. He was gonna cheat on his wife with a twenty-one year old fast ass girl who happened to be his friends daughter in an unknown location in the backseat of his car. Was it worth it?

Just then an unpleasant image of Rion in her mismatched bra and old maid panties popped into his head and he decided it was very much worth it.

As Tina spouted spellbinding driving directions Glen imagined her bellowing seductive commands when he was inside of her. By the time they made it to the secluded destination he was ready to cum by the sheer excitement of his thoughts. He was lucky he didn't need Viagra or Extenze at his age. "Think about your wife in fuddy-duddy panties," he demanded his dick. He didn't want to cum too soon.

The private spot was pitch black. Tina reached up turning on the interior car light. "That's too bright, sweetheart." Glen squinted.

"Well, it doesn't have a dim switch and I want to see you," she said alluringly moving from the passenger seat to straddle his lap.

"What if you don't like what you see?" Glen asked in earnest.

"I already like what I see or I wouldn't be here."

"My wife doesn't like it." Tina moved in closer and the smell of McDonalds french fries and Michael Kors perfume was oddly intoxicating to Glen.

"I'm not your wife," Tina stated firmly reaching for his zipper. Glen grabbed her hands. "Don't say I didn't warn you," he said in an apologizing tone.

"Relax," she sweetly ordered as she began to unzip his slacks to

reveal his solid, rigid, hairy penis.

"I don't see a problem. It looks delicious."

"Take a closer look," Glen told her. Tina pushed his seat back so she could fit between his legs and laid him back to recline so she could inspect his erect penis. The grey hairs seemed to glisten before her eyes.

"Baby, all you gotta do is get some Betty for Men if these lil' grey hairs bother you so much."

"Damn! Am I the only person who hasn't heard of this Betty shit?" he yelled with amusement.

"Check this out." Tina cleverly maneuvered her pants off to reveal a red thong. She then slid her panties to the side to reveal purple pubic hair. Glen laughed hysterically.

"I use Sexy Betty. You like?" she asked swirling her pelvis.

"Get in the back seat," he commanded her with a little extra bass in his voice.

"Yes, sir!"

Glen and Tina's relationship went on like this for almost a year. By that time Glen and Rion's savings account was down $56,485. Rion and Glen hadn't had sex since before the box of Betty for Men was knocked off the kitchen table and they were barely speaking to each other these days.

Rion noticed Glen seemed lively on Thursday nights when he supposedly went to play cards with his friends including Leroy, Tina's father. He had an extra swag that she was unfamiliar with. Tonight was his night out with the boys so she decided to pretend being interested in spending quality time together to see if he could be swayed to change his plans.

Rion purchased a box of Fun Betty and used it to create cute little hot pink hearts in her pubic hair to show she had a sense of humor about the whole thing.

She soaked in a hot bath, rubbed coconut oil over every inch of her body, put on her silver silk robe, and waited for Glen to get home. He arrived within perfect time from work and hit the shower immediately as usual on these special nights. The man didn't even bother to eat dinner when he got home.

When she no longer heard the water running in the shower Rion rushed to stand in the doorway letting her robe fall open. Glen almost slipped in the damp tub when he saw her.

"What the hell are you doing?" he asked grabbing a towel to dry himself. He didn't give her pink pubic hearts or the rest of her glossy body any attention.

"Look at me!" she dictated. He paused and gave her a once over. He began to laugh hysterically.

"What's so funny?" she asked vexed.

"What's up with the hearts, Rion? Is that from the Betty Love Collection?" he continued to laugh. Rion let her robe drop to the floor. He was naked and wet. She was naked and oily. What to do?

She moved in closer to him and wrapped her arms around his waist from behind. Her body heat was tempting him and his wet body caused their skin to connect. They both stared at each others reflection in the foggy full length bathroom mirror.

"Remember when we used to like each other?" Rion chimed. Glen shamefully looked away. She turned his body around to face her.

"What happened to us? You're more excited to be with your friends than you are to sit and have dinner with me."

Images of Tina started to cloud Glen's mind. "I can't do this right now. We can talk when I get back," he stammered attempting to get away. Rion grabbed his arm.

"Do you really think that if you leave this house without giving me some attention right now that there will be a later for you and I?" He was caught in a trap.

Their eyes met and their bodies moved closer by nature. Glen's penis was surprisingly stiff. For the first time in more than a decade

ELDERLY AND EDIBLE

Rion and Glen embraced and fell into an awkward kiss.

Kissing and hugging turned into grabbing and sucking and that turned into fucking and poking and on and on it went until they climaxed in the bed they once coldly shared. Tonight even the neighbors could feel the fire. Rion immediately fell asleep afterwards, but Glen made it a point to stay awake to call Tina and apologize for not showing up.

No answer. He knew he had fucked up. He was usually her ride home from work on Thursday nights. He sent her a text and a tweet, still no response. Tina must be livid.

He stood in the doorway of his bedroom and watched his wife of thirty-five years sleep peacefully. He thought about everything they had been through over the years - the miscarriages, the stalker, the fire. He decided his unanswered calls were the perfect opportunity to end things with Tina. He knew he couldn't keep going on like this. He had to shit or get off the pot.

He called Tina once more. This time he left a very long, heartfelt message informing her that he would like to see her one last time, but only to end their relationship respectively in person.

At the moment Glen was leaving Tina a message, she sat blankly staring at her phone, crying frantically. She did not go to work because her period was two weeks late. She had a feeling she might be pregnant, so she went to Planned Parenthood for a pregnancy test. Based on her sexual behavior it was suggested that she also be tested for STDs. They came back with a positive result for both pregnancy and HIV.

Tina listened to Glen's message and it was all the ammunition she needed to swallow a bottle of sleeping pills to end her and her unborn child's life.

Tina's pregnancy and HIV test results lay next to her lifeless body when she was found the next evening by her father. Word spread quickly about Tina throughout the community and the local news even created a special segment on her life and the effects of HIV in the black community.

Glen was wrecked and clearly hurt by Tina's death. He blamed himself but he was also afraid of what his own HIV status may be. He was too afraid to tell his wife about their relationship and quite frankly if he was HIV negative he would never tell her a damn thing. Rion and Glen had patched up a few holes in their marriage and they were having sex quite often. Glen decided to be tested immediately. Unfortunately, he was also HIV positive.

Rion knew about Glen's affair with Tina and was also being tested. She was given the OraSure test and would have to wait a week for her results.

Tina's father had been raping her repeatedly since age 11 and was not concerned with his HIV status. He continues to have unprotected sex with his wife, Tina's mother.

Glen was given the OraQuick test and received his results within twenty minutes. As he sat in his counseling session the news was too much for him to take. He suffered a fatal heart attack and died in front of the entire Planned Parenthood staff.

PAST
LIFE
BLUES

"Johnny and I both know that
we must take responsibility for our
actions or lack thereof.
It's not like we live in a world
that doesn't inform us of various
ways to practice safe sex."

I believe I was a white woman in a past life that obviously done some messed up stuff. Make no mistake I love being black. I love my sepia skin, coiled hair, broad nose, and ample ass, but I also love white men.

I suppose it would be more accurate to say I like this particular white man seeing as how he's the only white man I've gone to bed with. Would you believe that he has the biggest dick out of all the men I've ever had sex with? Stereotypes are not always based in truth.

Anyway, I ran up on the wrong white man and now I have HIV. I was negative before I met Johnny but when I was tested a year into our relationship, I was HIV positive. I usually got tested every six months, but my dumb ass got lazy and convinced I could never be infected. It's not enough to only know your status, you need to know your partners status as well.

I bitched Johnny out and made him get tested. He was okay until his results also came back positive. We were both devastated and Johnny threatened suicide. We were instructed by the Health Department to contact all past sex partners, tell them our status, and encourage them to be tested.

Many phones and doors were slammed in our faces, but one of Johnny's ex-girlfriends knew her HIV positive status. This angered us because she never took the time to contact Johnny. Was she hiding her status and spreading it purposely? There were also people that we were unable to contact. The Health Department took over the search from there.

Needless to say, it was all very tiring. I wanted to leave his side the moment I found out my status, but when you break it down, it takes two to tango. If both parties are unaware of their status and continue to have unprotected sex, this can and does happen to millions of people all over the world. I am not immune. I am not Super Woman.

Johnny and I both know that we must take responsibility for our actions or lack thereof. It's not like we live in a world that doesn't inform us of various ways to practice safe sex. The choice was ours. We made the wrong choice over and over again.

Over time our relationship has grown stronger. We speak at local schools and other HIV Awareness events and seminars together nationwide and we are living with HIV.

Johnny has been living with HIV longer than I have without proper care so he suffers more symptoms than I do. I saw some of these symptoms early in our relationship, but thought he had a cold or the flu. We both adhere to our HIV meds to keep our symptoms and T cells in check.

I forgot to mention that we travel as husband and wife. Hell yea, we got married! Why not? Both of us are infected. Who else would want to fuck us? Seriously, we love each other and wouldn't have it any other way. We don't have the same strain of the virus so we practice safe sex to reduce the risk of reinfection and the possibility of getting sicker.

During our public speaking engagements we often get bizarre stares and barbaric remarks mostly because he's white and I'm black, but it's quite a novelty for that fact. Black and White fighting together and showing the world that HIV is real and it affects us all. Folks always assume I infected him because black people have the highest infection rates in the United States, but Johnny is quick to set the record straight whenever we give interviews or are crudely asked who infected who.

The thing that boggles our minds the most are the numerous requests we receive to have sex. Sure, Johnny can slide on a condom and safely screw any woman he wants and I can have a man do the same except I'd be pulling out my dental dam. I love getting my pussy tenderly abused by a man's tongue and lips but those requests do not excite us.

Some of the folks who invite us into their bed even present handfuls of condoms and titty flashes to sweeten the pot. We've also been asked to join in group safe sex with other HIV positive people. The point I'm trying to make is that life and sex are not over because you're diagnosed with HIV, but having safe sex with countless others is not our mission.

It may sound strange but our life is more fulfilled because we know our status. Before, we took life for granted and lived carelessly. We made the decision to live life and be confident role models for people living with HIV. It's ironic that it took contracting HIV to make us see things clearly, but we know that what we're doing is right and we will keep on doing it until we've both succumb to this virus.

Sex with Johnny is positively fantastic. I think knowing our status has brought out the closet freak in both of us. We were kinky before, but now it's as if we're playing a game of Vulgar Idol.

Johnny won last round when he was able to get off by moving his dick back and forth between my big toe and the next. I won the week before by swinging my head over his dick and balls allowing my long dreads to bring him to climax. My dreads shone the next day and a week thereafter.

I've had an IUD inserted to prevent pregnancy. I do not want to risk bringing a child into the world HIV positive, though I could give birth to an HIV negative child if I took the proper precautions during my pregnancy.

We played around with adoption for about five minutes, one black child and one white child, but realized that our work would get in the way and that wouldn't be fair to the children. We also probably would catch hell from ignorant ass folks boycotting the adoption agency.

Most of our family is accepting, but there are a few that won't even hug or kiss us anymore. I want to tell them to kiss my ass. If you could get HIV from a kiss, hug, cup, or toilet seat it would be causing a bigger stir than all this silly ass H1N1 nonsense. There's no excuse for not knowing some basic facts about HIV/AIDS in this day and age, especially if you're fucking someone other than yourself.

We've accepted this type of slap in the face from our family and no longer attend events at their homes. These same people didn't particularity like us when we were simply known as the Jungle Fever couple, so quite frankly we're not surprised. We don't like their stankin' asses either.

People expect us to be mad, to give up, and to leave each other and die alone. Absurd! Look at Magic Johnson and Cookie. Magic is a very successful business man who is happily married with a family. That kind of life is not just for celebrities who live with HIV/AIDS. I'm sure Cookie weighed the pros and cons of being in a relationship with a man with HIV, but they made it work because they love each other. Love prevails and is more powerful than HIV will ever be. So, I guess I ran up on the right white man after all, damn that, I ran up on the right man.

I look forward to growing old with him and it is very possible that we'll do just that.

DATING DANGEROUS LEE

> *"Have your shit together, your teeth, your job, your mind, your car, your home, your laundry… if your shit is together you know what I'm saying."*

BY **L.A. LANGSTON**

I have known Dangerous Lee since birth. In fact, we were born on the same day at the same time at the same hospital. We grew up together and have been inseparable for more than thirty-four years. Let me help you to understand what makes her tick and what ticks her off.

Tip #1: HIV and STD free – This really needs no explanation after reading the last five chapters, does it? Be ready to get tested together before you get into her panties. It's good for your health.

Tip #2: If you're thinking of being her baby, it don't matter if you're black or white - It used to matter to Dangerous if you were black or white before she gave in to her attraction to white men. Her thought was that anyone who dated outside of their "race" was a self-hating individual. Dangerous Lee loves herself so her attraction to white men has nothing to do with hating her blackness. She likes men. Period. Quite frankly, she thinks they aren't all that different from one another and none are better than the other. Her non present white baby daddy is proof of this.

Tip #3: The less baggage the better – Dangerous Lee has a daughter and some emotional issues. Those are the two heavy items in her baggage. We all have baggage of some kind, but if your bags are overstuffed with several children, baby mamas and their drama, bad credit, bad breath or bad anything, stay away.

Tip #4: Single – Dangerous is sick and tired of married men and men with girlfriends pushing up on her. It's one of the main reasons why she is single. She is aware that monogamy is a lost cause for many people in this day and age, but please be honest if you're not into one woman at a time. Dangerous wants to let a ho be a ho.

Tip #5: Non Religious Liberal - If you're a stuffy judgmental conservative please do not step to Dangerous. You more than likely will not get along and she definitely is not going to church with you. Also, please have a sense of humor, a big one, don't be a goofy S.O.B. but be ready to laugh a lot and deal with sarcasm.

Tip #6: Have your shit together – your teeth, your job, your mind, your car, your home, your laundry…if your shit is together you get the point.

Tip #7: Don't try to change her mind – Dangerous doesn't want to be married and she doesn't want more children. That's not to say that there isn't a man out there who can change her mind, but don't hold your breath.

Tip #8: Nice ass please – She likes to have some ass to grab, slap, and admire. Flat or funny shaped assed men need not apply. In fact, Dangerous is very driven by physical attraction, but that's only in the beginning. Brains have to be a main ingredient.

Tip #9: Straight - Or be open about the fact that you like men. Just a few months before finishing this book Dangerous said that she would never date a man that liked to have sex with men or was attracted to men, but after learning about The Kinsey Scale and learning facts about sexuality she has changed her mind. Just be open and honest about who you are. Her response might shock you.

Tip #10: Don't let her writing fool you - She writes erotica, but that doesn't mean she's done everything that she writes about or even wants to. She wrote about a man getting off by fucking toes, but she has never experienced that. Would she be totally opposed? I'm not sure, but don't test this one. Ask her what she likes and she will tell you. Hopefully she asks what you like in return.

There's much more to learn about the complex and compelling Dangerous Lee, but I have given you a head start. Good luck fellas you're gonna need it!

HIV
FACTS

- HIV is only spread through blood, semen, breast milk, and vaginal fluid.

- HIV cannot be spread through urine, saliva, sweat, tears, or feces.

- HIV and AIDS are two different things. HIV is the virus that causes AIDS and AIDS can only be diagnosed by a physician.

- There is a window period between the time you have been infected and the time it takes the virus to appear in your system. In most cases it will take three months, in rare cases it can take up to six months.

- It is best to be tested for HIV every three to six months.

- Anal is the most dangerous form of unprotected sex, then vaginal, and lastly oral.

- During oral sex it is best to swallow vaginal fluids or semen immediately or spit them out immediately. Do not hold fluids in your mouth.

- If you're an injecting IV drug user and share needles, you're at risk for HIV.

- A woman with HIV can have a child that is HIV negative. She needs to take the proper medication during her pregnancy and have a cesarean delivery to help prevent the disease from spreading to her child.

- You cannot look at someone and tell they have HIV.

HIV FACTS

- You can be diagnosed with AIDS and get better, meaning your T cell count can increase, usually with the help of medication.

- You can have HIV for many years and have no symptoms.

- Symptoms of HIV are cold and flu like symptoms, night sweats, fatigue, diarrhea, and in women reoccurring yeast infections. These could also be symptoms of other viruses so please be tested to rule out HIV.

- African Americans and Latinos have the highest infection rates in the United States.

- People aged 13-24 have the highest new infection rates in the United States.

- 11 percent of all new HIV cases are in people over the age of 50.

- It is a felony if you have HIV and don't inform your partner before sexual penetration.

- There is no cure for HIV.

- HIV is preventable.

- If you already have an STD, you're at higher risk to contract HIV.

- Lube is a form of risk reduction. Water based lube is best.

- You cannot get HIV from insects, animals, or from casual contact, such as touching, kissing, or hugging.

HIV FACTS

- HIV is not a death sentence for everyone. It depends on the strain of HIV a person has, how much virus is in their system, how long they have lived with the virus prior to being tested, and how healthy or unhealthy of a person you are and the kind of lifestyle you lead that determines how the virus will affect you.

- The best way to prevent getting HIV is to use condoms for every sex act or abstain from sex and never share needles.

HIV
FICTION

- HIV is a gay disease.

- HIV is a white male disease.

- HIV was created by the government.

- There is a cure for HIV but the government is hiding it.

- There is a vaccine for HIV.

- HIV started because a human had sex with a monkey.

- HIV started because someone ate infected monkey meat.

- Birth control pills protect you from HIV.

- You can look at a person and tell that they have HIV.

- You can get HIV from a toilet seat.

- You can get HIV from sharing a cup.

- You can get HIV if a person with HIV touches a doorknob and you touch or lick the doorknob after them. (Sounds ridiculous, right? I got this one from a real life situation. It was asked by a teenager. Still want to keep your child in the dark?)

DEFINITIONS

- HIV – Human Immunodeficiency Virus

- AIDS – Acquired Immune Deficiency Syndrome

- Dental Dam - A thin piece of latex used to prevent the transfer of bodily fluids during cunnilingus or anilingus.

- Condom - A flexible sheath, usually made of thin rubber or latex, designed to cover the penis during sexual intercourse for contraceptive purposes or as a means of preventing sexually transmitted diseases.

- Female Condom - A device consisting of a loose-fitting polyurethane sheath closed at one end that is inserted intravaginally before sexual intercourse.

- Oral Sex – Sexual contact between the mouth and the genitals or anus; fellatio, cunnilingus, or anilingus.

- Anal Sex – Intercourse via the anus, committed by a man with a man or woman. Anal sex can also be committed by two women or woman to man using a dildo or vibrator.

- Dildo - An object that is shaped like and is used as a substitute for an erect penis.

- Vibrator - a vibrating electrical apparatus used in massage or for sexual stimulation.

- Semen - The sticky white fluid produced in the male reproductive system that carries sperm.

- Vaginal discharge - Secretions from the cervical glands of the vagina; normally clear or white

DEFINITIONS

- Sperm - A male gamete or reproductive cell; a spermatozoon.

- STD – Sexually Transmitted Disease

- STI – Sexually Transmitted Infection

- T Cell - any of several closely related lymphocytes, developed in the thymus, that circulate in the blood and lymph and orchestrate the immune system's response to infected or malignant cells, either by lymphokine secretions or by direct contact: helper T cells recognize foreign antigen on the surfaces of other cells, then they stimulate B cells to produce antibody and signal killer T cells to destroy the antigen-displaying cells; subsequently suppressor T cells return the immune system to normal by inactivating the B cells and killer T cells.

- Immune System - a diffuse, complex network of interacting cells, cell products, and cell-forming tissues that protects the body from pathogens and other foreign substances, destroys infected and malignant cells, and removes cellular debris: the system includes the thymus, spleen, lymph nodes and lymph tissue, stem cells, white blood cells, antibodies, and lymphokines.

- OraSure Test
  HIV antibody mouth swab test, requires up to 1 week to get results.

- OraQuick Test
  HIV antibody test, finger stick blood test OR mouth swab test. Results in 20 minutes.

THANKS

THANKS

- I want to thank ABC News for airing the television special *"Out of Control: AIDS in Black America"* that sparked my passion for the cause. I also want to thank my colleagues at Wellness AIDS Services, Inc. of Flint, Michigan. I have learned a great deal about HIV/AIDS and sexuality. I am a wiser person because of it. I love my job and what we do for HIV prevention and care.

- Thank you Hydeia Broadbent, Terrance Dean, and The King of Erotica for reading and reviewing stories. Your feedback was very valuable.

- Thank you Tunde Olaniran, Lisa Essett, and Timothy Jagielo for being an amazing photography team. Let's do it again!

- Thank you Dave Kudza for helping me with the layout and design of the cover and contents. Your work is the cherry on top!

- Thank you Mic Mountain for contributing the name Vashti to *"An Honest Ho"* and Tiffany McLean for contributing *"Pulse"* as the club name. Your input helped shape the storyline.

- Thank you Amanda (Mandie Sue) Emery for suggesting Michael Kors perfume for *"Elderly and Edible"*. I never wear perfume so I am totally clueless as to what smells good these days.

- Thank you Pharlon Randle of Bangtown Productions for giving this project a theme song.

- Thank you John Benjamin for creating an awesome trailer, always putting me in your movies and being there when I need someone to stroke my ego and gossip with.

- Thank you Tracey Whelpley for allowing me to use The Lunch Studio for my official book release celebration.

THANKS

- Thank you Zane for being an inspiring author and publishing my short story in your anthology. It's an honor.

- Thank you Eric Lillieberg for using your artistic talents to create merchandise designs.

- Thank you Rich Parsons for providing the swords.

- Thank you Monique Mensah for your editing advice on *"The Safe Sex Kit"* and Leigh LaForest for stepping in and editing the entire book.

- Many thanks to the creator(s) of Betty pubic hair dye. What an ingenious invention and great prop for *"Elderly and Edible"*.

- To the panties and bloomers that were destroyed for the purposes of this book cover and never got to serve their true purpose as an ass cover, I am very appreciative!

- To the underage kids who are going to sneak and read this book I hope you learn something valuable in the process. This book is for you too!

- Create Space, Blog Talk Radio, Word Press, Twitter, Facebook, MySpace, Hotmail, and Gmail. Without these services I would not have an audience or a way to communicate with them.

- I must thank all my Danger Babies for your support and attention thus far. I hope this book keeps you hooked. Love you!

- Very special thanks to L.A. Langston for always being there and being the sane one.

THANKS

- Special love to goes to my mom and daughter. You're my favorite girls in the world and I do this and all things creative to make you proud.

- Black people of the world - I wrote this book because I love you.

- I want to thank all the critics in advance that are gonna rip me apart and those that are gonna sing my praises. Both perspectives are necessary for me to thrive as a writer.

KEEP IT DANGEROUS

59